There's a Kid under My Bed!

Tales of Reggie the Monster

Written by
John J. Schmidt

Illustrated by
Evelyn M. Bergquist

Owl Canyon Press
Boulder, Colorado

Text copyright © 2021 by John J. Schmidt

Illustrations copyright © 2021 by Evelyn M. Bergquist

First Edition, 2021
All Rights Reserved
Library of Congress Cataloging-in-Publication Data

Schmidt, John J.
There's a kid under my bed—1st ed.
p. cm.
Hardcover ISBN: 978-1-952085-16-1
Softcover ISBN: 978-1-952085-17-8
Library of Congress Control Number: 2021950969

Owl Canyon Press
Boulder, Colorado

This Book Belongs to:

_____

There's a Kid under My Bed!

Tales of Reggie the Monster

Written by
John J. Schmidt

Illustrated by
Evelyn M. Bergquist

Dedication

To
Addyson
whose
creativity, humor and friendship
Reggie would appreciate.

Acknowledgments

I am delighted and honored that Evelyn Bergquist joined as illustrator for this inaugural tale about *Reggie the Monster*. Her whimsical and wonderful pictures helped bring Reggie, his family and other characters to life. I hope readers and others enjoy Ev's illustrations as much as I enjoyed collaborating with her.

Sincere thanks to Gene Hayworth and Keith Waters of Owl Canyon Press for their acceptance and guidance throughout this project. Gene's editorial expertise and production knowledge were invaluable, and Keith's continued support is much appreciated. Also want to acknowledge a friend, Darlene Feldick, who, after reading an early draft of this tale, prescribed Reggie's eyeglasses. An insightful suggestion!

As with all my books and writing projects, I am eternally grateful to Patricia whose love and encouragement bolster my enjoyment while pursuing these adventures. Her companionship and zest for life contribute so much to the creation of these characters and their stories.

—JJS

Rumble, rumble. Rattle, rattle. Rumpf, rumpf!
Reggie tossed and turned in bed.

"Reggie, what is going on?" his mom, Alva, called
from the living room.

"Go to sleep. You need to be rested for pre-school tomorrow," warned his mother.

"But Mom, there's a kid under my bed!" cried Reggie.

"I have told you, there is no such thing as children who hide under your bed!" Mom exclaimed.

"Would you like me to check under your bed?"

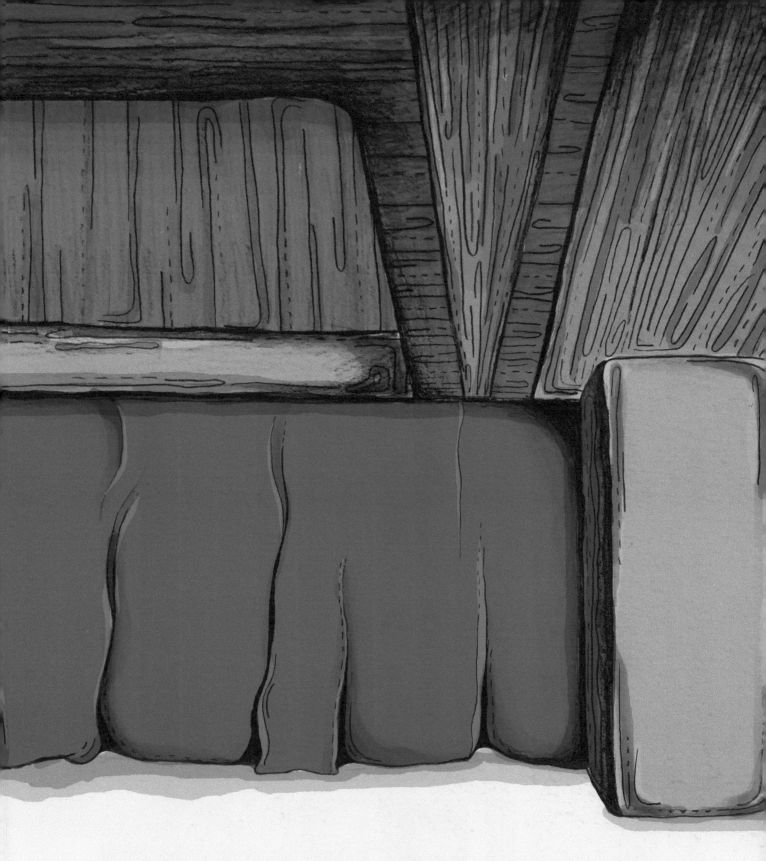

"No," pleaded Reggie as he looked under the bed while his bedroom door opened and Prissy, his older sister, peered in.

"What's up?" asked Prissy.
"Go away," he begged.
"I only want to help," Prissy insisted. "Are spooky kids bothering you again?"

"Yes. One is under the bed!" he shouted.
"I'll look," she offered.

"I don't see anything. Maybe it left when Mom called," concluded Prissy.

"Well a kid was under there!" Reggie asserted.

"I believe you, and I know why spooky kids hide under your bed," declared Prissy. "You do?" Reggie wondered. "Yes, it's this balloon bed skirt," she claimed. "You are too old for a babyish bed skirt. "

"You should ask Mom to get rid of it. Then kids won't hide under your bed! For tonight," she continued, "I'll tuck it under your mattress and the kid will stay away." "Now, take off your new eyeglasses and go to sleep."

"OK," said Reggie, as he put his glasses on the nightstand and fell asleep.

Next morning, Reggie and Prissy were having breakfast with their mother, Alva.

"After breakfast, Reggie," Alva said, "I will drive you to pre-school on the way to my salon." She owned a salon called Everything is Beautiful.

Their dad, Bud Scales, walked into the kitchen dressed for work. Alva asked, "Bud, do you have time for breakfast?" Bud managed a tunnel construction company called Tunnel Your Way Home. The Scales family lived in one of the many tunnels that made up their town of Tunnelville, outside the big city.

"Yes," Bud answered, "I would enjoy before they begin a new school year! Perhaps Prissy would like me to walk with her to the bus stop?" Prissy nodded with a smile.

After breakfast, everyone got ready to leave. Prissy dressed in her favorite purple jumper, which complemented her lavender body fur. Reggie wore a Planet Navigator T-shirt and jeans.

Prissy and Dad went to the bus stop.

As Reggie and Alva rode in the car to pre-school, he asked, "Will you take the bed skirt off my bed?" "I thought you liked it," she replied.

"I did, but I don't want it anymore."
"OK," Alva answered, "I can make a new one if you want."
"I'll think about it," said Reggie.

Reggie was familiar with Tunnelville pre-school because he visited once before with his mother. However, he had not met his new teacher nor other students, so he was a little nervous.

"I packed lunch for you, Reggie," said his mother.
"What is it?" he asked. "A sandwich, some Dragon Chips, and veggies," she answered.
"What kind of veggies?"
"No broccoli," she assured him. "Good," Reggie said with relief.

While Reggie and Prissy were at school, Alva worked at her salon.
"Reggie started pre-school today," she announced in the salon.
"Are you nervous for him?" one hairdresser asked.

"A little," Alva answered.
"Last night he was afraid there was a child under his bed!"
The hairdressers and customers laughed. "What imaginations these young monsters have," one customer snickered.

At mid-afternoon, Alva went to pick up Reggie.
"Tell me all about your day, Reggie," she asked. "It was fun,"
he replied. "Make any new friends?" Alva wondered. "Yes. I
met one who lives on Crater Street," Reggie
reported. "That's great!" his mom said.

"What did you decide about the bed skirt?" she asked.
"I want to take it off, but not put another on, yet,"
Reggie answered.
"OK," Mom said.

That night, Reggie got ready for bed. He put on his Planet Navigator pajamas and noticed the bed skirt was gone. He looked under the bed at the empty space. Nothing. No kid hiding under his bed. "Whew," he thought!

As Reggie climbed into bed, the door opened and Prissy peered in.
"Hi," she said, "I see your bed skirt is gone."

"Yes," answered Reggie. "Now a kid won't be hiding under my bed!"

"Wonder where it went?" asked Prissy.
"Where what went?" questioned Reggie.
"Why the kid, you silly!"

"What do you mean?" Reggie looked concerned.
"Well," responded Prissy, "if no kid is under your bed, I wonder where it went."
"Maybe it left and went to another monster's tunnel," said Reggie with confidence.

"Perhaps," she countered, "but I have heard that kids like to stay nearby."

"You mean it could still be here? But where?" Reggie surveyed the room.

"Maybe the closet," said Prissy. "It's dark like under your bed. Children prefer dark, scary places. Let me check."

"No!" begged Reggie. "I don't want to know."
"OK, but I thought I saw some eyes looking out," Prissy warned.

"Well, sleep tight," giggled Prissy as she left.
"But what if there is a kid in my closet?" asked Reggie.

"It may not bother you," responded Prissy, "since it is the first night in the closet."

Alva called from the living room, "Reggie, it's time for you to go to sleep!"

"But Mom! There's a kid in my closet!"
shouted Reggie.

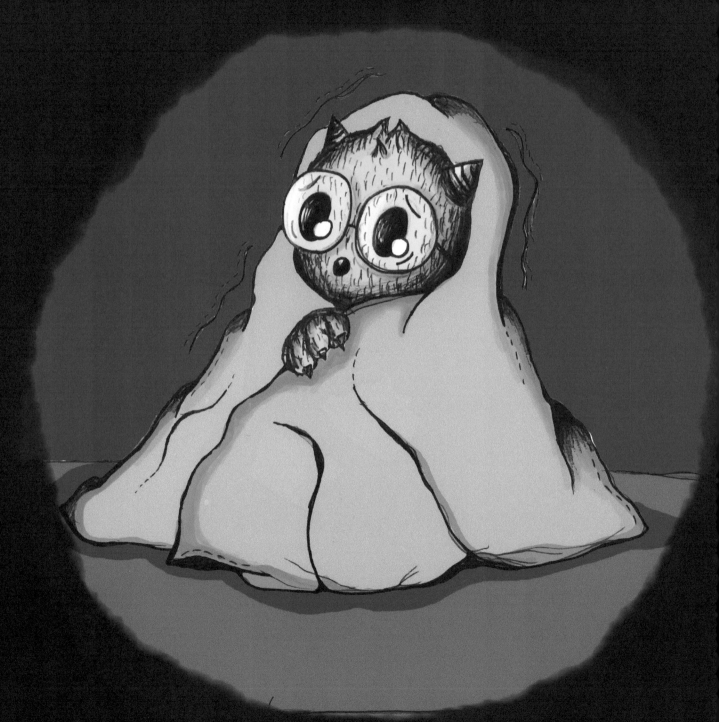

(to be continued...watch for the
next tale of *Reggie the Monster*.)

ABOUT THE AUTHOR

John J. (Jack) Schmidt has been writing for as long as he can remember. Beginning in high school as a sports editor, through college when he also was a sports editor for the newspaper and an editor of the college's literary journal, he went on to author and co-author more than 20 books and several professional articles throughout his career. In 1988, Jack wrote and illustrated a book about friendship for middle grade students. Later, he expanded it into a curriculum guide titled Making and Keeping Friends. During his career in education and counseling, Dr. Schmidt was a teacher, counselor, supervisor, and university professor. Now retired, he is emeritus professor of counselor education at East Carolina University where he headed the department for several years. This inaugural tale about *Reggie the Monster* is his first children's picture book, and he plans more tales about Reggie in the future. Jack and Patricia, his wife of more than 50 years, like to travel and spend time together. In addition to writing, Jack has enjoyed playing tennis, pickleball, golf, and the guitar through the years. He hopes you enjoy this story of *Reggie the Monster* as much as he enjoyed writing it.

ABOUT THE ILLUSTRATOR

Evelyn M. Bergquist is an emerging illustrator and print-maker. She recently graduated from Drexel University with a degree in Behavioral Health Counseling and a minor in Fine Arts. She has been drawing ever since she could hold a pencil and has been studying artmaking for several years. Currently, she works as an artists' assistant in a studio specializing in glass sculpture and screenprint. During her free time, she enjoys being with friends, spending time outdoors, and playing guitar with her band. This is the first book she has illustrated.

To order additional copies of

There's a Kid under My Bed!
Tales of Reggie the Monster

visit the Owl Canyon Press website at:

www.owlcanyonpress.com

CPSIA information can be obtained
at www.ICGtesting.com
Printed in the USA
BVHW022305311022
650806BV00002B/31